What I Learned By Not Killing People

Michael West

iUniverse, Inc.
New York   Bloomington

What I Learned By Not Killing People

iUniverse books may be ordered through booksellers or by contacting:

iUniverse
1663 Liberty Drive
Bloomington, IN 47403
www.iuniverse.com
1-800-Authors (1-800-288-4677)

ISBN: 978-1-4401-5384-6 (pbk)
ISBN: 978-1-4401-5385-3 (ebk)

Printed in the United States of America

iUniverse rev. date: 6/23/2009

My Business Dream

When I left the army, all I found were closed doors. I spent the next three months being told that I was a strong candidate, but unfortunately lacking in commercial experience. All I wanted was the chance to start afresh in the fast paced business world. I wanted to be one of those guys buying his coffee whilst talking on the phone, or maybe spending that precious lunch hour in the park with his steady girlfriend.

Instead I was left with no option but to do what I knew best. Killing people.

I'm not going to lie to you. The pay was incredible, even if the lifestyle was a little strange. I ended up moving into a nice little apartment in Florida. That's right. The American market was thriving in comparison to the one back home in England that was already dominated by two bit gangsters. You know the type. Think Manchester, ugly and beer drinking.

Ten or so jobs later and I moved to a nice little, yet fairly massive mansion, three minutes down the road.

Yes, life was certainly good. There was still something missing though. I had no office romance, and no one who served me coffee would recognise me or even ask how my day was going. The half normal life I was in search of just crept further away.

This was all until the month of May, 2009.

The Head Hunter

Target name: Josh Lozenger
Age: 34

Josh was no different from a lot of contracts that came my way. Like

1

any other man in his thirties he was prone to making the same mistake over and over again. Chasing the wrong woman.

He worked for the prestigious Bresner Deinkorn recruitment firm in San Francisco. By day, Josh could juggle up to three phones whilst eating lunch, sealing deals for top executives who all wished to jump ship to a better offer. This suited him just fine, because the better the offer, the better the pay day. Just like you might have gone through two chocolate bars, he would have made himself around ten thousand dollars before lunch.

By night however, Josh was as lonely as they came. He had enough money to buy any woman he wanted, but he had that all too common ability to lock eyes with the ones that were trouble.

Her name was Katrina Jung, a Swedish born girl with a taste for the finer things in life. Josh became obsessed the second he laid eyes on her across the busy gym. The beautiful blonde hair that was slightly matted to her forehead by a moist film of sweat, those slender legs that glowed like a quiet camp fire and the big green eyes that could read your mind even if it was obvious what you were thinking.

After another day of knocking everybody on their asses, Josh would settle back into his beautifully crafted office chair and begin the slow routine of shutting down his computer. Then he'd head on over to the mini bar and grab a cold Budweiser, loosening his tie and settling back into the reclining chair where he'd close his eyes and imagine taking Katrina to the opera, or a log cabin in Canada, where they would walk through the woods collecting firewood, and drink red wine in front of some old movies.

The one thing that was standing in Josh's way was the well known 'businessman' Harvey Johnson, the man who shared a bed with Katarina every night.

I still recall the drink I had with Harvey as we negotiated a deal. He was extremely frank about what he wanted.

"The last thing I need is some slimy head hunter making a mockery of my reputation, so this is how I see it going down. You wake up and find a substantial amount of money waiting for you at the agreed drop off, and then I wake up the following day and read about Mr. Joshua Lozenger being found head first in a meat grinder."

Harvey was as gay as they came. I knew that, and I'm fairly sure everybody else did too. There were rumours about his obsession with a young Persian man that he had set up in his own private house so they could spend time together away from the watchful eyes of Harvey's security detail.

A man like Harvey didn't terrorise the San Francisco locals by being seen with a younger man. He spent the evenings in the finest Italian restaurants and glitziest bars, with Katrina hovering at his side. For the occasional photo opportunity, he even placed the odd kiss on her full and voluptuous lips making every hetero sexual man within the vicinity cry slowly into their suddenly tasteless and warm champagne.

If Josh had gone after the girlfriend of a car salesman then maybe things would have turned out different. Instead he pursued the woman of a man who earned a crust by smuggling drugs, women, Polish mustard (a surprisingly lucrative venture) and guns throughout America. You didn't do that kind of a job without having a naturally ruthless streak in you.

"Just one more thing," added an irritable Harvey as he paid the bar tab. "I don't want any screw ups on this. Are we clear?"

"I'm a professional dickhead. You're lucky I'm even considering this."

Whilst Harvey tried to comprehend what had just happened, I left a tip on the bar and headed back to the Californian sunshine, eager to return to the plush hotel and its vast array of free bathroom products.

As I showered and thought about the meeting, I wondered whether it would be worth investigating other lines of business now that I was in town. California seemed to have so much more going on than back home in Florida and I still had the secret dream of the hustle and bustle game that everyone else liked playing so much with their meetings, brain storms and team building retreats.

After showering I dried myself off and threw on some clothes, smart casual and designer, perfect for a lone stroll on a Friday night. Not forgetting my to-do list, I sat myself down and scrawled a quick postcard home.

Dear Mum,

How are you? San Francisco is beautiful and there are lots of places to see. I'm just heading out now for a walk and a meal. I'll try and stop by a museum and see if I can improve myself!

Send my love to everyone,

Michael.

I sat three tables away from Josh Lozenger, who was dining with an attractive looking brunette. It was clear that this woman was more interested in him than he was in her, but over the course of my remarkable pasta dish I was impressed at how well Josh sat back, listening as she poured her heart out. She probably thought she was falling in love at that very moment.

As Josh stood up to go to the bathroom I quickly went through the plan in my head once more. *Follow, kill and leave.* I rose from my chair as eloquently as possible, and glided towards the double doors in the corner of the restaurant. This would be a little public, but with enough….

"Are you okay?"

I quickly got back on my feet, a little shocked at the speed of the man who'd sent me crashing to the ground.

"I apologise, I didn't see you. Can I get you a glass of water or something?"

It was Josh Lozenger. I couldn't believe it. I'd found a head hunter with manners.

"Thank you, I'll be fine."

He wouldn't let it go.

"At least let me buy you a drink, you're sitting in the corner right?"

I nodded slowly.

"I'll have it sent over, and don't worry, I'll be more careful in future okay?"

He wore a playful smile and I realised he was expecting some sort of reciprocation, which I gave him in my most playful voice.

"Next time I'll give you a ticket!"

We both laughed and went our separate ways. I stood in front of the bathroom mirror and wondered what had just happened. When I returned to my table, there was no sign of Josh and the girl, but there was a fresh Budweiser waiting for me on my table.

A head hunter who kept his word. This was turning into a strange night.

The Next Morning

"What the hell is Josh Lozenger doing still alive Michael? I was told you were the best!"

My coffee was only a six out of ten. This was not the morning I'd hoped for. Now I had this scum bag giving me an earful about my failed assignment.

"He'll be dead by the end of the day Mr. Johnson. Can I get another coffee? This one's a little lame."

Harvey shouted something in Spanish to a man who hurried away before turning back to me.

"You'd better not be fucking with me Michael."

"You know what, forget the coffee, I really have to get going. Just make sure the rest of the money finds its way towards my account."

I excused myself and jumped into the strange Hybrid vehicle I'd rented. My new idea had me so excited I didn't even care about the lack of caffeine.

As I drove through the impressive gold gates of Mr. Johnson's mansion, I thought about how sweet it would be to punch him, just once, to see what happened. I had to fight that urge though, mainly due to the significant pay cheque I had waiting for me and to keep my professional reputation at the highest standard the underworld had come to expect.

"Good morning. Michael West to see Josh Lozenger."

The receptionist at Bresner Deinkorn looked doubtful, so I prepared my next line which I knew was bullet proof.

"It's really very important."

She picked up the phone and made the call. In minutes I was being shown along the immaculate corridor that took me past room after room of phone monkeys, all jabbering away like a scene from Wall Street. Josh had his own office up at the end, and I wondered just how much jabbering he'd had to do to earn it.

Josh looked surprised as I sat down across from his power seat.

"Hello Josh."

"You? What..I mean, how.."

"How do I know your name and what am I doing here?"

"Yeah."

I understood his caution.

"Josh, Katrina doesn't feel the same way you feel about her. I know she's devastatingly attractive and would probably do all kinds of crazy things in bed but it's just not going to happen. Ever."

I saw heartbreak creep across Josh's face and for a few seconds he was like a small boy who'd been screeched at by his mother in the middle of a busy shopping centre.

"You don't understand."

"No, you don't understand Josh. I'm being paid four million dollars to kill you by the end of the day."

Five Hours Later

"Just a gin and tonic please," I smiled, as the beaming hostess took away my empty cup.

Flying first class was truly the way forward. Josh didn't seem to concur, snoring away beside me as a result of the extremely strong sedative he'd taken. It didn't surprise me that he was scared of flying, most people were, especially slender guys in suits. Not that he was particularly slender, just that he had the sort of…feminine vibe about him.

I'd given Josh some simple home truths. First of all I'd guaranteed him protection from Harvey Johnson, which he was going to need. Secondly, I'd assured him of a room in my impressive mansion back home.

All Josh had to do in return was teach me how to be more like him. A successful businessman.

I dropped Josh off at home and hit the streets once more. I thought having some space would do him good and give him the chance to get to know his surroundings. Meanwhile I was off to pay a visit to my good friend Alan, the accountant.

My Accountant

"It's all here Michael. Four million dollars give or take a little on the tax."

"But it's a lot of money right?"

"Yes, you'll be sleeping with a roof over your head for a little while longer. Dare I ask where this fortune came from?"

"Another dead relative."

"You have so many these days."

I jumped up off the sofa and made my way to the smart sliding glass doors of Alan's therapeutically quiet office.

"Thanks Alan, say hi to your wife."

"Michael, I've been divorced for three years now."

"Oh yeah. Okay, take it easy."

Knickers. I kept forgetting about Alan and his divorce. Poor bastard. I made a point to write it down this time, lest he began to feel I really didn't care about anything he had to say.

Josh was watching an NBA game with my best friend Heidi. Heidi was a nice, predictably normal Labrador who had been given to me as a present from Alan's ex wife.

I only hoped I wasn't pushing him too fast, but I was already approaching the dreaded forties and my career hadn't even started.

"Josh, I need you to sit down and look at my resumé. I'm going to go and catch up on my e mails for the next ten minutes so if you could just write some notes for me we'll reconvene over some tea."

That should be manageable, I thought to myself, opening up my hotmail account to check the good news. I had a new one from Harvey Johnson.

I hear Joshua went missing from work recently (hehe). Good stuff Mikey!

What a prick. Now he was calling me Mikey. I wondered just how long it would take for him to find out the truth. Two days? Two years?

There was one from Amber, a librarian I'd been on a few dates with.

Hey you! It's been awfully quiet around here without your presence. Any plans for the weekend?

I had a lot of plans for the weekend. Amber would have to wait, which was a little annoying considering the stuff she got up to in the privacy of her own home, away from the monotony of her life in the public library. Maybe she would make a good girlfriend. I would have to arrange something with her in the next few weeks.

There was just one more e mail that caught my eye. To the untrained average Joe it was just another piece of spam offering up beneficial treatments for your winky.

To the trained eye of a good looking assassin it was another request, no different from someone e mailing a radio station with their favourite song. Well there was a slight difference in that instead of playing a song, I was expected to kill someone.

The Call Girl

Target Name: Cherry
Actual Target Name: Katie Deline
Age: 22
Actual Age: 26

"Why do you need this girl dead Penelope?"

I always liked to know what I was getting myself into, and as I looked across the table at the composed woman in front of me I couldn't help but wonder why she wanted to ice some call girl at my extortionately high rate.

"Do you know what a Madam is Michael?"

"A pimp disguised as an attractive and sophisticated lady?"

It was supposed to be a joke but it went down like a lead balloon. For a moment I worried about losing the contract.

"I'm sure you understand how serious it would be to my professional existence should my little black book go missing."

I thought about it. This was America, the internet was in full flow and reality was being distorted at a higher rate than ever. Her little black book was probably worth millions of dollars in clients alone, and who knows what kind of preferences they had behind closed doors.

"Say no more Madam."

And she didn't.

I was left on the hotel veranda with my mango juice and a brown envelope containing the customary half of the bill up front. Madam Penelope was a ruthless one, but I had to admit, fairly attractive in her determination.

Back at home I found Josh yapping into the telephone.

"Lozenger, Josh Lozenger, I'm just a friend of Michael's."

Josh paused and slowly put down the phone.

"He hung up."

"Who hung up."

"I don't know, some guy. He was looking for you but you weren't here two minutes ago so I was trying to take a message."

This was very bad. I never gave out my home number for obvious reasons but there were some clients who had longer arms than others.

"Josh, don't ever answer the phone in this house okay?"

"No problem Michael. I'm sorry."

"Never mind. What did you make of my resumé?"

Josh had obviously thought about this, his brow was furrowed like an architect wondering what made his new building collapse after one hour.

"I think you need to ditch the resumé."

"Why?"

"It's something I've been thinking about at work. I mean, who wants to read three pages of lies and exaggerations?"

"Go on."

"Well, you said you're interested in the digital industry? Online marketing and such, am I right?"

"That's right."

"More and more employers are looking for people who have an understanding of how the digital world works, or at least an online presence. So the way I see it, you should begin by starting your own blog online and use that to showcase your talent or whatever it is you've got to offer."

I liked his angle. It seemed I'd underestimated Josh. He was thinking outside the box, even if he was a little slow in other ways such as not answering my damn phone.

"Josh, I like that idea a lot. So that's one step out of the way. Now listen, I have to head out and take care of something are you going to be okay here?"

The phone rang. Josh reacted like a ninja.

"Josh Lozenger speaking."

He hung up as quick as he answered, realising the error in judgement.

"Jesus Michael, I'm sorry. I guess it's kind of embedded in me."

"It's not too hard to grasp Josh. Don't answer the phone."

He looked down, but I didn't have time to lecture him. I was already running late.

I found Katie Deline, or 'Cherry', entertaining a particularly ugly man at a smart wine bar in the centre of town. The man was getting a little far ahead of himself and his hands were wandering very persistently up Cherry's leg resulting in an agitated Cherry pushing them away, only seeming to amuse her client even more.

I watched with interest wondering why a little touching was a problem when he was probably going to do a lot more in some hotel room down the road. Maybe there were set rules in this game, certain do's and don'ts that this particular client had trouble understanding. I can't say I blamed him. She was one exceptionally attractive girl who subconsciously screamed at you to touch her. I knew that whatever line of work she chose in life that power alone would be enough to get her a long way.

After another five minutes and round of drinks the happy couple got up to leave and it was time for me to do what I did best. Stalk.

As I drove I wondered about starting an online blog. I wasn't a complete idiot, I knew the world was changing and so called 'bloggers' were no longer viewed as narcissistic, socially retarded, inexperienced loners, but it didn't change the fact that I had nothing to blog about, bar being a pro hit man.

The happy couple parked outside an expensive looking block of apartments that I remember looking at when I first moved down here. I believe the main issue I had was with the location, a little too far from the beach which meant no chance of hearing the breaking waves every morning. I loved the sound of the sea in the morning, it reminded me of absolutely nothing but it still sounded blissful.

I watched them enter the building and slowly checked my weapon. Everything seemed fine, now it was just a waiting game. The waiting game lasted only seven minutes, as Cherry appeared back down on the street, striding off towards town. What the hell was going on? I pulled a u-turn and accelerated after her.

"Excuse me? Excuse me Miss?"

She turned and looked in admiration at my sports car. I'd almost forgotten how sweet it was myself, and for a moment I felt like Jerry Springer but I wasn't sure why.

Maybe he had the same car and I'd read about it somewhere.

"Can I help you?"

She thought I was a potential score. No wonder Penelope was mad at her, branching out on her own without sharing any of the proceeds.

"I'd like to think so. Hop in."

And just like that I had a fresh faced blonde in the front seat of my Jerry Springer sports car. If only things were that easy in my teenage years, instead of begging girls for their phone numbers at the taxi rank.

"Hey maybe you should slow down? There are cops around you know."

She was right, but I wasn't going to slow down. For one thing the blast of air was helping me clear my thoughts, and furthermore, I was actually driving Cherry home to kill her, and I didn't want any unnecessary questions.

"Hey wait a minute, where are we going? Do you live this way?"

I kept silent and sped up. Cherry knew better than to make a scene, and I was confident she had no experience with exiting a moving vehicle. We pulled up outside her modest but extremely well kept house. I already knew her friend Kirsty was out of town for the weekend so there would be no disturbances.

"Cherry, we need to go inside and get that little black book that belongs to Penelope."

Cherry tensed up. She almost looked scared.

"That bitch. I made her more money in the last year than she'd seen in the last five."

"Yeah, well I'm sorry about that. C'mon let's go."

She marched over to the safe which was hidden behind a painting of an old man performing what appeared to be some kind of martial art. Although I wasn't impressed with the unoriginal hiding place, I was taken aback that Cherry had the need for a safe. It was very forward thinking, considering her tendency for theft.

"Here you are. Now what? Are you going to kill me?"

No one had been this up front with me before. They were usually shaking or talking nonsense. Some just cried. Cherry became impatient with the waiting.

"Look, if you're going to do it, just do it."

Nike had no idea just how good their slogan was.

"You're not scared?"

"No offence, but you seem more scared than me."

My God she was right. I wasn't focused at all. A part of me wondered whether Josh had spilt anything on my sofa, and the other part was still wondering why Cherry had been so quick with her client.

"Why were you only upstairs with that man for seven minutes?"

"Do you really want to know?"

"Yes."

"He pays me ten thousand dollars to lock him in a cage over night."

"So you have to go and let him out tomorrow?"

"Well sure. But I can't do that if I'm dead."

Ten thousand dollars. A little black book. If I didn't know any better I'd have said the girl in front of me was on to something. If ever there was a time to make a snap decision based purely on instinct then it was now, as I held a gun in the face of this tough little blonde.

"Come home with me. We'll find a way to sort this mess out."

"Do I have a choice?"

And so we drove off towards the safety of my own home, the sea air ruffling both of our hair respectfully as we most likely pondered just where the hell this situation was going.

Back at the base, Josh was panicking about something.

"Michael, Michael, I don't know what or how, or what…"

"Spit it out Josh."

"The dog, I mean, Heidi…she just exploded, all over the floor, I mean, it's everywhere!"

I hadn't noticed the smell of fresh dog whoopsie on entering the room but it wasn't long until the odour powered up my nostrils. Cherry took the word right out of my mouth.

"Gross!"

"Who's this Michael?"

"Cherry. Meet Josh."

The pair of them waved at each other awkwardly and I knew I was going to have to make an extra effort playing host.

"Josh, Cherry will be staying with us for a while okay?"

"Were you supposed to kill her like me?"

"Pretty much. Why don't you two help yourselves to the beer in the fridge, I'll take Heidi outside for a quick walk."

I took the dog outside for no other reason than to let Josh and Cherry become a little more comfortable with each other. As strange as the last few days had been, I felt that I was on to a winner with this new form of erratic thinking.

Instead of wasting two fairly innocent individuals, I had put them up at my house and started the foundations of my new, completely normal life.

As Heidi did her business on the lawn I started to consider the ramifications of keeping the two new guests in my house alive. It was most likely that someone would turn up eventually to try and kill us all but I figured that I had at least a week or two before it came to that. Maybe longer considering the economic climate and how fees were going through the roof in my line of business as more and more hit men quit the game to find something more meaningful.

Two Weeks Later

The system was working. I was waking up at seven every day and wandering downstairs to find Josh already making the coffee. We'd chat about the previous nights' sports scores, whether it was NBA, NFL, English football or tennis, it didn't matter. This was male bonding time, but without the beer.

At precisely eight fifteeen, Cherry would appear in a silk dressing gown, having failed to completely shake off her sleep but looking all the cuter for it. My time with Cherry happened nearer eleven, which gave her enough time to shower, preen and do whatever else it was that women did in the morning.

I then quizzed her for a few hours over what I liked to call 'niche seduction' which I knew there was going to be big money in. 'Niche Seduction' simply meant the more unusual requests that Cherry had received from her clients such as the man in the cage who she did remember to release the night after I met her.

It made me think that almost everybody in the world was slightly weird but they just refused to show it. What if I could offer them some kind of safe haven to exist in their dream alternate reality without it upsetting the rhythm of their normal lives?

The cogs in my brain were slowly turning, a little more every day, and with Cherry and I throwing the ideas back and forth, it was reassuring to know that when the plan did finally come together, I would have one of the best salesman working from my own home.

Better yet, I didn't even have to pay a wage, as technically, the reward was life itself. However, I knew that if the business started to succeed I would financially compensate my new employees. It was only fair.

That night I went on a date with Amber the librarian. We went to watch some movie about a guy whose girlfriend cheated on him but then found a better girl across the street which made the original girlfriend jealous and win him back for one night which made the new girlfriend slightly heartbroken and move to Arizona after which the guy followed her and begged for forgiveness only to find his original girlfriend was about to die from an aneurysm. It was quite good but I didn't think I'd buy the DVD when it came out.

After that we enjoyed some ice cream by the beach and I started to wonder whether she was going to invite me back to her place or not.

"Michael, I've been thinking."

Oh no.

"I really like spending time with you, but sometimes I'm just not sure whether you feel the same way."

"That's crazy Amber," I said as my phone started vibrating like mad in my pocket. It was Adam Hazard.

"It's okay Michael, you can answer it."

"Thanks," I said, grinning sheepishly, genuinely a little embarrassed at having to interrupt her when she was talking about her feelings.

"What is it Adam?"

Adam was a long term friend and fellow underworld contact that saw, smelt and heard pretty much everything along the west coast.

"Harvey's on to you Michael. I don't know how he knows but he knows everything."

"Including where I live?"

"Yeah, that too."

"Thanks Adam."

"Anytime pal."

I hung up and turned back to Amber.

"Amber I'm so sorry about that, just business building up. It's pretty non stop right now."

"It always is Michael."

And that was when I knew I had to pull out the big guns, not literally speaking.

"I know I've been a little distant Amber, but that's not because of you, I promise. I'm just scared of moving along too fast without really knowing who you are, or what it is you want."

She was listening.

"Look, I know this sounds corny, but there are times when I feel like if I have to go to one more bar or restaurant in a shirt I would never dream of wearing, to impress a girl I hardly even know......"

Cue long and drawn out sigh with head slightly lowered. Raise head and hold strong eye contact.

"All I really want to do is just cuddle up with you on the sofa and watch a little quality television. Is that a crime?"

Amber took me by the hand and marched me towards the street whilst simultaneously hailing a taxi. On the short journey to her apartment I sent Josh a quick text message.

Josh. Not back tonight. Lasagne in the fridge, should b enough 4 u and Cherry. Pls lock all doors and set alarm. Seriously. Michael.

I hoped that just one night away would be okay.

The following morning I approached my mansion with some degree of caution that proved unnecessary when I heard the sounds of Cherry and Josh playing tennis. So, unless it was Harvey and Cherry playing tennis with Josh's head it was just another day chez Michael.

On the subject of Harvey I decided to sit Josh down and have a little talk with him.

"Cherry's really something isn't she?"

"Josh, you're not listening to me. There's a very strong possibility that Harvey is going to come after you, and probably me."

"No I understand Michael, this is what I do to distract myself from the reality of the situation."

I had guessed that myself but I also knew he was developing a crush on Cherry. She was the new Katrina.

"Look, you don't have to worry too much, I can handle Harvey."

I actually wasn't sure whether I could handle Harvey because I had no idea how he was going to exact his revenge. If it was just him turning up at my place then yes, I could probably handle it. If it was a team of highly trained killing machines then I'd probably still be okay but there was a definite risk of myself and everyone else dying in a horrible way.

My train of thought was interrupted by a text from Amber.

Thinking about u. xxx

Nice, but a little bit much. I needed a coffee.

"Josh you couldn't rustle up some of your world famous coffee could you?"

It was time to create a 'to do' list. I grabbed a pencil and paper as Josh busied himself with my futuristic Italian coffee machine.

- Find out what Harvey's doing- might have to pay Adam Hazard
- Make time for Amber- slow things down or dampen her interest somehow
- More dog biscuits for Heidi
- START NEW BUSINESS!!!!

The final point was really giving me a headache. I knew if I didn't just get going with something then it would be another six months and I'd still be in exactly the same place. Besides, all I'd done was kill people so whatever I chose to do next was always going to be a step up no matter how impractical it was.

"Here you go."

"Thanks Josh."

Damn he made a good coffee. But I didn't have time to enjoy it like I usually would.

"Josh, get Cherry in here would you?"

Five minutes later, the three of us were seated at the kitchen table and I prepared to make my pitch.

"Okay you two, here it is. Dream Awake."

"What's Dream Awake?"

"I'm glad you ask Cherry. Dream Awake is a small agency that specialises in making your deepest fantasies come true no matter how unrealistic they may be."

"You mean like a Mistress or high class escort?"

"It doesn't have to be of a sexual nature. If Tom from Oregon wants to fly to Hawaii and pretend he's there to surf in the Rip Curl tournament then we will make it happen. If Sally from New York wants to handle a press conference regarding her new film, then we will make it happen."

They both looked at me. I was vulnerable.

"I think I like it Michael," said Josh slowly.

Cherry slowly nodded her head too, and gave her input to the conversation.

"If Brad from San Diego wants to be treated like a big shot lawyer for a weekend in Paris, we can make it happen!"

And so it happened. Dream Awake was born. Cherry and I would do the creative thinking and handle the contacts which we expected to be either from the seedy world of sex or the seedy world of powerful people, two groups that Cherry and I were extremely familiar with. Then we would unleash Josh like a rabid pit bull, and it would be sell sell sell all the way, with non stop business development and tough negotiations.

The tricky part would be the marketing.

Hey Harvey

With all our notes scribbled down furiously on a never ending supply of printer paper we all decided to take a little break before we killed each other.

Cherry opted for a book in the garden, while Josh chose the home cinema for a bit of escape time. I went straight into town to check out some of the latest marketing magazines. I planned to buy at least eight, and spend the next few hours skimming through them and using the best five ideas as a way to market Dream Awake. I wasn't certain this method was how all the great ventures began but I didn't have any better ideas.

"How's it hanging Michael?"

I didn't recognize the chunky ruffian standing next to me. He was flicking through a sports magazine but I got the impression he wasn't the least bit interested.

"Do I know you?"

"Harvey sends his regards."

The man smiled, and turned to leave. The plan was to scare me of course but I wasn't Josh Lozenger. In fact, this was a fantastic opportunity to take control of the situation before it got out of hand.

I followed the man outside. He probably thought that a threat in a public place offered no chance of retaliation but he was mistaken. Statistics showed that members of the public were far more likely to ignore an act of violence for fear of being hurt themselves.

I grabbed the man by the collar and spun him round, ramming my fist straight into the bridge of his unbroken nose.

"Tell me exactly where Harvey is and I promise that will be the only inconvenient thing that happens to you today."

The stunned man knew I was serious, and his voice shook a little as he tried to force the words out.

"Th- th..there's a café ..just…he's in a café two blocks down, that way. Café Rosa."

I pushed the man away and headed quickly towards the destination. If I could surprise Harvey, I felt there was a chance of resolving the situation with no further violence. I had the perfect idea.

"Hey Harvey, don't get up."

He was unsurprisingly a little surprised to see me so soon into his travels. Like a true professional, he managed to hide it well.

"Michael. What a surprise."

"We need to talk Harvey."

I called the waiter over and ordered a plate of fries before continuing.

"Josh Lozenger is no longer a problem to you and I think you know that. This is about pride, and I can understand that of course. In a way, I screwed you over."

"That's putting it mildly."

"Maybe, yes."

I went for the kill.

"What if I was to tell you that your secret little urges were more possible than you thought?"

"What are you talking about?"

"I'm talking about no more limitations. No more running away to that bolt hole with the Persian boy. No more watching your back like a jittery closet gay person."

"I still don't know what you're talking about."

Christ. Some people are just unbelievable.

"You like men Harvey. I know it. It's my business to know it. I know you pretend to enjoy pottery because that Persian boy likes it and you know that if you didn't play along he'd just find another millionaire to look after him."

The truth can hurt some people, but others tend to be surprised by the sudden relief of being exposed. Harvey knew I was right. He was also unnerved about my knowledge on his movements and the fact that his henchman hadn't returned from delivering his threat to me. On the basis of this, he sat back and decided to hear me out.

"So what are you suggesting?"

And so I told him all about Dream Awake. As an act of good faith, Harvey was guaranteed a twenty five percent discount on all our services. He was amazingly mellow in comparison to his mood before I pitched to him.

"You know Michael, I've been considering moving operations here for some time now. Dream Awake might just be the catalyst I needed to get things going. I can't promise I'm fine with letting Josh Lozenger off the hook but I'm a reasonable man."

What a ridiculous cliché. This raving homo was lucky I hadn't just killed him and saved the inconvenience of our conversation. But I did need my first client for Dream Awake and Harvey was most definitely a whale.

"I think we understand each other Harvey. I'd like to apologise once more for the slight glitch in our previous agreement."

Harvey nodded, and pushed a card across the table.

"That's my private number Michael. Call me in a few days and we can meet to discuss business. I'll be in town for a few weeks."

"I look forward to it."

I turned to leave but had a quick thought. I didn't want this Godather feeling too cosy in my company.

"Just one more thing Harvey."

"Shoot."

"If anyone threatens me again in my home town I'll take two of your toes and feed them to you. Or beat the shit out of you. Whatever."

He'd probably like that though. What a freak. I jumped in the car and sped off, Heidi would be needing a walk and I was sure Cherry and Josh hadn't bothered to move since I'd last seen them.

I pulled in through the gates to find Alan the accountant waiting outside the front door.

"Alan, to what do I owe the pleasure?"

He looked uncomfortable, almost squirmy. Something was bothering him.

"Michael. I uh…"

"Come inside and tell me all about it. I'm thirsty."

I led the way into the kitchen and grabbed two bottles of ice cold beer from the fridge.

"I've got a few problems with Lucille."

"I thought you guys were divorced?"

"No Michael, I'm divorced from Clarissa. Lucille is my girlfriend."

I drew a blank. Dammit, I needed to remember these things. Alan was probably the most important man in my life considering my sheer ineptitude with numbers.

"Lucille! Of course. I'm sorry Alan, it's been one hell of a morning. So what's the problem?"

"She's kicked me out of the house."

"That's a big problem Alan."

Could I really allow another body into my mansion? I was only just getting used to having Cherry and Josh around and now I had to put up with my accountant? Deep down I knew there really was no choice.

"Alan, you stay here as long as you need okay. Take the bedroom in the east wing, sixth door on the right just after the bathroom."

"Michael, I don't know how to thank you, honestly."

"Alan, please. You're my accountant and I love you for that. Plus, I actually might need a lot of advice from you over the next few days and this will save me the drive to your office."

"Okay then."

"Great. Excuse me a second, I'm just taking Heidi for a quick walk round the block."

I left Alan looking somewhat useless in the kitchen and returned to the sunshine with the dog in tow. As we breezed past old ladies on their power walks and the odd teenager practicing rubbish skateboard tricks I tried to think of some fantasies that might keep Harvey amused.

Now that Alan was living with us it would probably be a good time to set up the financial support for Dream Awake and discuss the various ins and outs regarding the legal issues of starting a new business. I'd never felt so alive, not even the days of parachute jumps and bombs could compare to this beautiful business rush. Maybe I'd wear a suit every day.

Back at the mansion I found a flustered Josh.

"Michael, I just went into the bathroom and there's a stranger sitting on the toilet!"

"Relax Josh. That's Alan, my accountant. He's the final piece of the Dream Awake jig-saw."

Upstairs we heard the simultaneous sound of Cherry screaming and Alan gasping apologies.

Dream Awake

"Okay, what have we got this morning Cherry?"

"A couple from Phoenix want to do the White House package, so we've booked it in for next week."

"How long for? One week? Two?"

"They're going with the five day package."

"Well, it's a start. That's ten thousand after tax. Are all the actors taken care of?"

"Signed and sealed, one had to drop out but I'm waiting on a replacement to get back to me."

"Fine."

The White House package was a popular little product of ours which allowed any person or persons to be the President for a small period of time. Using my real estate contacts we were able to replicate the Oval office using a warehouse downtown and both Cherry and Josh worked hard on finding the right actors to make the experience all the more real.

Customers could even choose the goings on during their imaginary time in office and whilst some opted for a peaceful term, others were keen to go with high level threat situations such as an imminent terrorist attack on the country.

For the latter choice especially, it was absolutely vital to find the right kind of actors, specifically those with stage experience and a natural ability for improvisation.

"Josh, how are we looking with the new business?"

"I've managed to agree a one month trial period with Brent Technologies which allow their employees use of our services at a fifty percent discount."

"I'm not so sure about that to be honest Josh. It's all well and good getting a new client on board but what are the chances of them retaining our services after the trial period?"

"Well it's a technology company so there are a number of lonely individuals on the workforce with money to spend. I genuinely believe that these are the people we're aiming for and if they enjoy the experience enough then we're looking at a long term commitment."

He was good. Almost too good. I'd have to keep an eye on Josh and make sure his ideas didn't better mine. Although it was common knowledge that most CEO types surrounded themselves with brighter people, I wasn't so sure I wanted to be outclassed just yet.

"Michael, I need to take a few minutes with you to go over the finances."

"It's okay Alan, you can talk freely in front of everyone."

"Well, I'm concerned about cash flow. It's important to get a customer or a thousand before you jump. I'm not saying sell your product too cheap as a lot of people go bust making sales, but there's a fine balance. You're better to have a sale and some money, than no sale at all. Keep your expenses to those you must make."

And that was why I loved Alan. Everything about him was so boring and so deliciously necessary.

"Relax Alan. I understand what you're saying but you forget that aside from my small fortune which I'm prepared to invest, I can always take on some part time contracts of my own to bring in a little extra."

I was fairly sure Alan knew about my killing people but I didn't think it wise to open up too much about it. Deep down I hoped that I would not need to kill anyone again and the business could survive on its own, but if it was a case of sink or swim then someone was getting a bullet between the eyes.

"Alright, listen up everybody. Great work this morning, let's take a few hours to ourselves and Cherry, I will need to spend a quick fire twenty minutes with you discussing Harvey."

"Okay."

"Great. Let's reconvene back here at three o'clock."

Josh and Alan organised their various sheets and folders before heading off to unwind in the palatial garden and I escorted Cherry to the study so we could come up with something concrete for Harvey.

Harvey and I had spent a great deal of time on the phone together before I realised that he was far more comfortable expressing his desires to a non threatening female. As a result, I'd handed over all of his business to Cherry who as well as having a great deal of experience with sexual desires was far better at bringing Harvey out of his shell and into the comfort zone.

Overall, Cherry had spent at least ten hours on the phone with Harvey, continuously going over his options and trying to form some kind of package. Eventually they settled on a ten day package at twenty thousand dollars that entailed a retreat somewhere north of Las Vegas.

In the interest of good taste and confidentiality I can't go into great detail but it involved five Dutch steel workers, a game of croquet and plenty of costumes.

Josh managed to forge a good relationship with a Hollywood studio that allowed us full use of their costume and prop collections which was ideal for Dream Awake and due to the financial difficulties in their industry it meant that we only had to pay a small retainer.

It was all about seeing the opportunity and exploiting it. For all his innocence, Josh was born with that killer instinct so few people have. In different circumstances, he would have made an excellent soldier.

So that was Harvey well and truly in my pocket and out of my things to be worried about list. I still had to think about Amber, and possibly Madam Penelope who had been awfully quiet since I'd not killed Cherry. That reminded me.

"Alan!"

I shouted from the bottom of the stairs, suddenly feeling very on edge.

"Alan!"

Alan came rushing from his room.

"Yes Michael."

"Have I been paid any money in the last forty eight hours, say, maybe three million dollars?"

"No of course not Michael, you know I would have told you something like that."

"I know you would have Alan, no harm done. Sorry for the panic."

Shit. That stupid wench hadn't paid me the rest of money which meant she knew Cherry was still alive. Or that she was a cheap skate. But if she knew that Cherry was still alive why hadn't she called me with a complaint?

"Michael there's someone on the phone for you. A lady called Penelope? She's really rude I might add."

"Josh I told you not to answer the phone. Put it through to the study."

Well this should be interesting I thought to myself, gliding into my power chair behind the solid oak desk.

"Penelope my dear, how are you?"

"You little scum bag Michael. Did you really think I wouldn't notice that dainty tart was still alive?"

Just play it cool Michael. Method acting is the way forward.

"Penelope, what are you talking about? I put the girl on ice, just like we agreed."

"Then why did she queue jump me in Starbucks this morning?"

Damn. I'd told Cherry to keep to the house as much as possible for the first few months.

"I'll give you a million dollars if you let this go without a fight Penelope."

"I want a million dollars and a meeting. I know you're up to something."

"Fine. But I want a guarantee that I have nothing to worry about."

"As long as you're at the steak house on the corner of Westleigh at two o'clock tomorrow afternoon then you have nothing to worry about."

She hung up the phone, and I rushed to find my 'to do' list. My new life running a business was becoming ever more complicated. The management magazines had warned me about multi tasking.

I'm Sorry Madam

I sat down with the immaculately dressed Penelope and tried as best I could to explain the turn of events that had let me to not only accommodate Cherry, but also a random head hunter and my accountant.

"Dream Awake?"

"Yeah. Dream Awake."

"That's an odd name for a business."

"You might say it's an odd name for an odd business!"

I laughed but Penelope didn't.

"I want a stake in the business."

"Then I want all your sex industry contacts at my disposal."

She looked confused. I elaborated.

"Dream Awake offers personal and private fantasies with full discretion. Considering that the average customer is going to be someone who has an unfulfilled sex life then I think it's safe to say that for you to part own some of the business I'm going to need a little help in boosting revenue."

"That little slut already has the black book."

"It's only got names from A through to F. I'm going to need the rest of the alphabet Penny."

"Let me guess. You take all the details and have your little salesman run business development. Am I correct?"

She was correct, and, like Cherry, she was a complete natural. Maybe in time I'd have another employee, but it was clearly too soon to push that angle.

"Yes, that's correct."

"Then I want twenty percent."

"You can have the million dollars and five percent."

"Fine."

Wow. It was easier than I expected. I'd heard that women entrepreneurs had a much lower business failure rate than their male counterparts. The main reason was that they usually didn't think they knew everything, and weren't afraid to just ask people for help. That didn't seem to apply to either Penelope or Cherry but it was an anecdote I constantly tried to keep at the front of my mind.

Back at home I enjoyed a game of Monopoly with Cherry, Josh and Alan. It was the perfect setting to break the news about Penelope, but of course I knew it wasn't going to be easy selling the idea to Cherry. That was why I had Josh do it.

The problem was obvious. I was about to risk losing Cherry's trust and friendship by entering in to a business relationship with the woman who had paid me to kill her.

Cherry and I had formed a dynamic working relationship and I certainly didn't want to see that break down. As for our personal relationship, I don't think there was any doubt we had a connection. So it seemed relationship was the word of the day. Was I prepared to risk my relationship on every level with this remarkable call girl?

"Josh, I need to know that you can make this happen."

Josh and I had snuck away from the Monopoly festivities and we stood in the narrow laundry room through the back of my spotless kitchen. The smell of sirloin steaks still hung thick in the air, and I wondered if it would attach itself to the designer shirts I had drying on the rack.

"Can't you just kill Penelope? That's what you do isn't it?"

"Josh, I am both shocked and appalled. Is that what you've become now? You're a head hunter, where are your morals?"

"I'm sorry Michael, but this is going to be a tough sell."

And so we sat down on the floor of the laundry room and used a pen and paper to solve our problem.

I'm Sorry Madam, Part II

24 hours later and with no successful answer to my Penelope/Cherry issue I called on Josh once more, to join me in the laundry room. We covered our tracks by telling Cherry that we were taking care of laundry in bulk as it seemed more economical and took a different approach with Alan by telling him to just mind his own business.

Alan was the accountant, nothing more, and I didn't want him rising above his station. Intimidation was key.

"Okay Josh, let's put this to bed. There's no way in hell we can have Penelope joining our team."

"I agree."

"But it would be nice to have the rest of the alphabet from her little black books."

"Yes. What do we have at the moment?"

"We have A through to F."

And so we devised the plan of the century in ten minutes, and it was up to Josh to sell it to everyone. A few seconds before he gave his presentation to the rest of us I grabbed his papers and told him to sit down.

It was rude of me but at the last moment I had realised that I couldn't risk Josh getting the credit for this one.

"Sorry to rush you all in here guys but there's something we need to discuss."

I began to tell the story about my meeting with Penelope and her proposal. As expected, Cherry reacted badly to the news.

"Are you fucking kidding me?"

I was immediately relieved Josh and I had come to the conclusion of not allowing Penelope into the fold, because judging by Cherry's outcry things would have become very sticky.

"Cherry. Sit down and take a deep breath. Of course we're not considering taking her on, the thought never crossed my mind."

Cherry sat down, but there was no deep breath. She was fuming. I needed to come up with the goods or I risked the whole existence of Dream Awake. I took a slow and purposeful sip of my water, shuffled some papers, cleared my throat and began the presentation.

Operation Screw Over Madam

The operation was simple. I was to call up Penelope and arrange a meeting somewhere in town. Josh would accompany me as a sign of my sincerity in bringing Penelope on board and Alan would head over to Penelope's house with Cherry.

I had already prepared and written a downloadable e-book on breaking and entering which was made available to Alan at a small price of nineteen dollars.

Alan and Cherry would use the e-book to make a clean entry into Penelope's house at which point they would locate the necessary black books and make copies.

The beauty of it was that Josh, Penelope and I would be having celebratory drinks just five minutes away. What Penelope wouldn't know was that we would be secretly celebrating her demise as the number one fulfiller of fantasies in Florida.

"Michael, are you sure it's safe for us to just break in?"

"That's a good question Alan. First of all, Josh and I will be with Penelope, so that puts her out of the picture. As for security, all I know is that she's employed a burnt out cage fighter by the name of Hernando. From what I can see, all he does is the occasional patrol of the grounds, and smoke a pipe in front of Seinfeld re-runs."

Alan didn't look convinced. I knew I had to win him over.

"Look at me Alan. You'll be fine. The e-book will tell you everything. There's even a little section on hand to hand combat in the unlikely event of a confrontation. If that fails, then Cherry will take care of him."

Cherry nodded. She was as cold as ice, secure in the knowledge that no matter what the threat, it could always be eliminated by a simple showing of flesh and her dancing eyes.

I knew this all to well, but we needed all the help we could get and Alan was an integral part of the operation even though he was pretty much useless at everything except for being an accountant.

It was settled. I looked everyone long and hard in the eye, leaving no room for any chicken shit thoughts.

"We leave in an hour."

I'm Sorry Madam, Part III

"Alright you two, hop out."

Josh had parked on the south side of Madam Penelope's property and it was time for Cherry and Alan to depart on their journey. They were both clad in black, armed with bags of supplies and, of course, my e-book on breaking and entering.

Josh and I continued to the front gates where we were buzzed in. I marvelled at the wonderful garden furniture Penelope had going on and by the time we'd pulled up outside the front door I'd already settled on a couple of small statues for my own place.

"Good evening Penelope. This is Josh Lozenger."

"A pleasure Josh," said Penelope, climbing into the car.

We drove away, and there was no sign of security. I didn't assume anything, and I hoped that Alan had been over my e-book enough times to feel comfortable.

At the restaurant we all chatted about the state of the welfare system and various upcoming sporting events from around the globe. Penelope was an avid Lakers fan and was understandably nervous about the upcoming playoffs.

Josh chewed quietly on his beautifully cooked salmon and I toyed with my garnished steak. I was probably eating a little too much steak in general but the iron was ensuring I was alert at all times.

"Penelope, this is somewhat awkward, but I'm afraid I've had to reconsider your proposal regarding Dream Awake."

"Excuse me?"

"I can't allow you to hold any kind of stake in my company Penelope. It's just not an option. I'm sorry that I've had to do this."

Penelope lunged to her right. I couldn't understand. I was sitting to her left. Then I heard the yelping sound of a dog that had been stepped on by a clumsy owner. Only there was no dog. The howl had come from Josh. It was at that point I knew one of the most unimaginable things had just happened and threatened to ruin my whole plan.

Penelope had grabbed hold of Josh's testicles.

For what seemed like an age Josh writhed in a slow and mesmerising display of anguish and agony. I was caught in two minds. Rescue Josh and ruin Dream Awake, or leave him and return home?

"Let go Penelope. I'm not joking."

"You think I'm fucking around Michael?"

Her voice was a low hiss, inaudible to any of the other diners who ignored our unfolding drama. Josh wasn't going to last much longer. His hands were clenched, fists resting in the middle of his salmon dish and his face was turning a deep purple.

From somewhere within his mouth came a quiet gurgling noise.

"Jesus Christ Penelope, let him go. You're crushing his testicles!"

"Give me my share Michael."

Penelope made a large twisting motion and Josh fainted. I made my move, knocking the table out of the way and diving into the psychotic Madam, bundling her to the floor. The table crashed to the ground and our five star meals spilled everywhere, as the onlookers gathered in amazement.

Penelope screamed and clawed at my face. She was like a cat on acid and I struggled to keep her under control.

Josh was curled up a few yards away, simulating the foetal position. I didn't know if he was going to make it. I screamed at one of the gawping diners.

"Get that guy an ambulance!"

As Penelope clawed away at my face I slowly and purposely wrapped my thighs around her uncannily slim waist line and squeezed. Our faces pressed together and our eyes locked. I'd never been so attracted to anyone before which was ironic considering I was patiently squeezing the life from her writhing body.

"Forgive me Penelope," I whispered as I heard the last rush of air leave her. It was only the second time I'd killed somebody in that way and I thanked my stars that I'd made the effort to watch 'Goldeneye', Pierce Brosnan's debut Bond flick from 1995. Or 1996, but that was splitting hairs.

I rolled away and tried to catch my breath. The last two minutes had felt like an eternity and I could hear the wail of sirens in the distance. I needed to get out and quickly.

"Michael! Over here!"

That voice. I couldn't believe it. It was Harvey. He was parked outside in a spanking new car that screamed class.

"Come on, get in!"

I stumbled across the small and tacky garden that separated the restaurant from the street, and within seconds I was being sped away by the worlds' most feared gangster.

"You're one ruthless son of a bitch Michael, I'll give you that."

Harvey was almost smiling, as he weaved in and out of the heavy Florida traffic. I didn't say anything. I just watched the road fly by and thought about Josh and his poor testicles.

The Cover Up

"Good job you two. Good fucking job."

I was a little on edge as a result of the earlier excitement. I needed a stiff drink. Alan and Cherry sat in front of me with copies of Penelope's black books.

"How did the dinner with Penelope go, and who's this guy?"

Cherry had every right to ask questions, she had just risked her life for the sake of Dream Awake.

"I'm not going to lie to you Cherry. The dinner could have gone a lot better. This is Harvey. I believe the two of you have spoken over the phone in quite some detail.

"Gosh, Mr. Johnson, I had no idea. It's so nice to meet you."

Harvey stepped forward.

"The pleasure is all mine Cherry. I'm ever grateful for the hard work done by you and Dream Awake. Who's this guy?"

Alan hadn't said a word.

"That's Alan. Don't worry, he's just the accountant. Why don't we head on through to the living room?"

I walked Harvey into my palatial family style living room and sat him down.

"Can I offer you a drink? Beer maybe?"

"I'm fine thanks Michael. Let's not waste any time, we need to cover your tracks."

Harvey was right. The police would be asking questions and Josh would be trapped in hospital receiving treatment for his swollen, torn or possibly severely bruised testicles. Harvey reassured me.

"They'll be fine. I've had my testicles in a vice for two hours before and they recovered remarkably."

"How long did it take?"

"About a month. But that's a small price to pay."

Harvey was right. Josh would survive, but I needed to get him out of the hospital.

"As for Penelope, you just leave that to me."

I liked the sound of those words. Something told me Harvey was used to handling this kind of scenario. Despite his short comings, he was remarkably composed under pressure. If life had led him another way, he'd have made an excellent sales man.

Little did I know that Harvey's men were already rampaging through Penelope's house, planting drugs, child pornography and weapons in all the places a police unit would search, and search they would.

It was superb. Penelope wasn't murdered in a freak incident at the restaurant. She was now a victim of her own doing, a woman in so deep with the criminal underworld her death was yet another blessing and reason people could feel safe at night.

"What about the witnesses?"

"What witnesses?" smiled Harvey, counting through his endless stream of green bills. Uncle Sam had come through for me. God bless greed and desire.

That night I said a prayer for Madam Penelope. I had learnt that business was not too different from killing people.

The Fast Company Review

A month had passed and things were really falling into place. Josh's testicles had made a full recovery, and he was even able to cross his legs again when reading the Sunday papers.

Cherry had stepped up her game with Dream Awake, taking care of a multitude of clients ranging from Technology companies to retired Baseball stars. Whatever the problem, Cherry's quick thinking and smooth talking found the solution. Nothing was out of reach in her eyes.

Alan was number crunching like a man possessed, happy to be distracted from his disastrous romantic life, and in Josh, he had found a friend that possessed all the qualities he so sorely needed.

Josh himself was happy to mentor Alan on the art of confidence and salesmanship, and by simply recovering from his testicle disaster and launching himself back into work he was setting a wonderful example.

Then came our biggest break. Much respected Business magazine Fast Company reviewed Dream Awake in time for us to make the front page of the December issue.

It was something that was beyond my wildest dreams, and it was only then that I started to consider myself to be an official entrepreneur.

Dream A Little Dream Of Me- how Michael West is fast becoming the real life genie for millions of Americans.

Article by Gloria Wynsham.

With his disarming charm and retro looks, Michael West is not someone you'd expect to be running alongside some of today's most innovative business men and women. When I first met him, I thought I was being introduced to some typical PR schmoozer and prepared myself to be bored to death about up and coming micro trends or internet niches that were going to change the world.

Instead I was left in awe as I chatted to this rather quiet and considerate individual who calmly explained the necessity of his new venture 'Dream Awake.'

"We live in a world so starved of reward, where people are made to feel insignificant in the face of celebrity and power that the end result is a mass of embittered men and women who feel as if they have been shunned."

Michael's answer to this dilemma? Dream Awake. A service that provides you with any dream you can imagine. Literally.

"It's been incredible," continued Michael. "The response has been over-

whelming and we feel so lucky to be able to provide these customers with dreams they thought were so out of reach. It all comes at a price of course."

So what are these dreams exactly?

"We've done everything from accommodating couples in their very own French castles, where they can re-enact their lives as the King and Queen from allowing teenagers to line up on the basketball court and play a full ten minutes in the NBA."

So how can Dream Awake pull these strings?

"Business connections are frightfully important and our small team are very lucky to have met and worked with a wide variety of exceptional individuals. Between the four of us we have a number of friendships with some of America's most prominent entrepreneurs who not only offer support in terms of financial backing, but also invaluable business advice which is just a God send for a newbie like myself."

Dream Awake is heavily reliant on its well trained actors to enable a realistic fantasy to all of its clients and there is the occasional rumour of it being nothing more than a 'high class escort agency'.

"It is true that we have had clients who opt for an adventure that leans more towards the adult side of things but we certainly don't discriminate against any requests as this would be hypocritical. Clients are offered complete discretion if they wish, or alternatively they can create a free blog online that acts as a reminder of their fantasy to show their friends and family."

And with a smile, Michael West excuses himself, extremely apologetic to be leaving me after only an hour.

"It's these damned meetings with my accountant. If only I'd listened to my maths teacher in school!"

Something told me that Michael West was probably going to get away with his lack of numerical skills, and good luck to him.

Visit the Dream Awake website at www.dreamawake.com.

The article marked a serious chapter in Dream Awakes' short life. I knew that within days we'd be bombarded with orders, and I had to prepare for the onslaught. At that moment I received a text from Amber.

Everything ok? Haven't heard from you for a while x

Knickers. I'd forgotten about Amber. I made a note to ask her out for dinner and headed to the meeting room.

"Morning guys," I said, breezing past the seated Cherry and Alan who already had their coffee and pastry.

"Michael. We've got a problem."

"What is it Cherry?"

I had a feeling I already knew what the problem was. Following our recent exposure by Fast Company it was expected that the volume of calls would increase one hundred fold.

"90% of our latest clients are seeking services of a sexual nature. If it carries on like this we'll be no different than any other brothel."

I knew Cherry was upset. During the rise she'd been pioneering a daring new business model that was gaining the following and respect from seasoned professionals such as Richard Branson and kitchen utensil genius, George Foreman.

Now, there was a very real threat of Dream Awake becoming nothing more than a seedy motel for single computer engineers and divorced insurance brokers.

Josh had been uncharacteristically quiet. I hadn't even noticed he was in the room.

"Josh, how are your balls?"

"Much better thanks Michael."

"You seem awfully quiet. Is everything okay?"

Josh shifted uncomfortably.

"We lost Mango Inc this morning. They didn't give a reason."

Mango Inc had been one of our best clients, and their requests were never of a sexual nature. They were probably the one company that kept our reputation intact and the main reason Fast Company even considered writing about us.

"Cherry, get on the line with Marcus over at Mango and get to the bottom of this. Alan, see how much it's going to cost us if we lose Mango as a client. Josh, you come with me. We're not done just yet."

I marched out of the room with Josh and relayed my new plan of action.

"Josh, I need you to set up another company today."

"Another company?"

"Relax, it's going to be under the Dream Awake umbrella, but it will cater only for adult entertainment."

"So we won't lose our main source of income."

"Exactly. And once that headache is over we can sit back and bust a gut growing Dream Awake as an official non sexual fantasy safe haven.

Any demands of a sexual nature will simply be routed through to our second company."

"What shall we call it?"

"The House of Discretion."

"I like it."

I knew Josh would like the name. It was bulletproof.

"I knew you would. Move all House of Discretion operations to our renovated lofts in the South West. I'll leave Cherry in charge of the décor and staffing. Now let's move, I need at least fifteen employed Mistresses by the end of the week."

House of Discretion vs Dream Awake

So I was now running two separate businesses. Alan, Cherry and Josh were being worked to the bone. We were all tired. But we were all getting very, very rich. My life was starting to come together.

Cherry used all of her call girl friends for the day to day running of House of Discretion which was three floors of beautiful Victorian style mansion in the south west of the city. In reality, it was no different to any other brothel but with Madam Penelope six feet under and her black books in our possession we cornered the entire market within a month.

As for Dream Awake, it became something of an admin nightmare. With the majority of business heading in the direction of House of Discretion I was working Josh extra hard to try and push some new non sexual business towards Dream Awake

It was a date with Amber that proved to be the turning point.

Having unintentionally ignored her following our previous date I managed to find a spare two hours and take her for a round of crazy golf. During this time, as I rediscovered the joys of feeling ten years old again, Amber started an interesting conversation about her fellow librarian, Marvin.

"He just sits there all day playing on the internet before heading back to his Mother's house."

"His mother? How old is this guy?"

"Forty-five. And stinking rich. His Daddy owned a franchise of Chunk Burger."

"Chunk Burger? There are over seven million of them on the East Coast alone."

"I know, it's an impressive number. Would you like to play this last hole and then visit the new art gallery? I've been waiting ages to go."

I wasn't going to be going to any art gallery. It was time for a little old fashioned snooping.

The New Client

With Harvey happily settled in the ways of our House of Discretion it was no surprise that Dream Awake was suffering financially. Until Amber had dropped the information regarding her co-librarian, I had considered myself in a desperate position.

That was no longer the case, and as I laid the last of my phone taps in Marvin's house, I knew it was only a waiting game. In under an hour I had placed cameras, listening devices, a phone tap and internet tracking software in Marvin's pleasant apartment.

I only had a short window of time as his Mother had left for Bridge, and I knew she'd soon be heading home after stopping off for her regular bottle of red wine.

I then returned to Amber's apartment to make sweet love to her and explain why I had run off following our round of crazy golf. I didn't technically explain, so much as I lied, but the end result was a great two hours for the both of us.

Later that night, I told Josh, Cherry and Alan about my day.

"Sounds like a big fish, he just needs to find the bait."

"Well we'll know what the bait is just as soon as my intel comes in. I think a few days should be enough to gauge exactly what he's looking for."

And how right I was.

In those few days Marvin had placed over one hundred calls to the Matthew Fox chat line. Furthermore, his internet results showed an unhealthy interest in the television series LOST. He'd browsed over five hundred fan sites and had even started three of his own that mostly revolved around the purpose of the island.

It seemed that he wasn't so much interested in Matthew Fox the actor as he was in his LOST character, Jack.

I gave the information to Josh and left him a few hours to devise the strategy. The end result was a fully integrated digital marketing campaign that saw a lot of carefully worded ads finding their way to Marvin's internet searches as well as two letters posted directly to his apartment which described just some of the services offered by Dream Awake.

Dream Awake has provided its clients with services from a day in Rio de Janeiro to a week spent being Matthew Fox from LOST.

I admired the bluntness of Josh's approach. We could have wasted thousands listening to various 'consultants' and attending free seminars but at the end of the day all you needed was a little (and I really mean little) imagination and hard work.

One week later and we still hadn't heard anything. I was getting frustrated. The three million dollars from our whore house eased the pain slightly but I wanted Dream Awake to fly. It was time to pay little Marvin a visit.

Would The Real Marvin Please Stand Up?

I flicked the cigarette right into Alan's lap, and his delayed reaction cased him a minor burning sensation on the lower stomach area.

"Christ Alan, I'm sorry. That was meant to go outside the car."

Alan composed himself.

"It's fine Michael. Just to double check, why am I here again?"

"Josh is tired."

I hadn't planned on taking Alan as my accomplice but Josh was a little tired and I didn't want to put Cherry in any kind of danger considering just how much money she was making me every week.

After not hearing a peep from Marvin following the aggressive marketing campaign I was eager to find out just exactly what had gone wrong. Not one for faffing around I came up with the suave plan of asking Marvin himself.

In a few minutes I'd picked the lock and Alan and I were moving inside and down the hallway. I'd already made sure the Mother had left for her Saturday morning golf leaving it highly likely that Marvin would be surfing like a mad man on the internet.

And there he was. Podgy, red haired and with a slight odour that reminded you of a small boys locker room.

"Don't move fat boy."

I kept my gun trained on Marvin.

"Who the hell are you? What is this?"

"Relax Marvin. Just want to ask you a few questions and then we'll be gone. This is Alan by the way, my accountant."

Alan looked panicked but I had to interrogate Marvin whether it was legal or not.

"Why haven't you contacted Dream Awake?"

I was surprised at the speed of his response.

"I don't like to leave the house."

"What about when you work?"

"If I didn't have a job, Mum would kick me out."

"Aren't you worth somewhere in the region of a billion dollars?"

"Mum doesn't let me have it."

This had been a huge waste of time. I took a moment to think.

"Can I use your bathroom?"

"Anything, anything at all. Just don't kill me, please."

I noticed the strong smell in the room and assumed Marvin was sweating a little harder than usual.

"Alan, watch him for me."

I gave my glock nine millimetre to Alan and headed for the bathroom.

Sitting down on the toilet I flipped through a series of clever political animations and tried to plan my next move. It was as I washed my hands that the answer came to me. Marvin was an internet nerd. I could find out what he responds to online. If you need answers, you have to ask questions.

Rushing back into the room I couldn't contain my excitement. I grabbed the gun of a worried looking Alan and pointed it at the even more worried looking Marvin.

"Marvin. You're Mother won't be back until at least eleven-thirty. Tell me absolutely everything I need to know about successfully marketing a product on the internet!"

For the next ninety minutes Marvin filled us in on the complexities of the internet. I made a list of interesting angles that were worth looking at.

- PPC Marketing
- Google adsense
- Digg.com
- StumbleUpon.com
- Twitter
- Facebook
- Myspace
- SEO Optimization
- E mail marketing
- Blogging

- Viral marketing
- Podcasting

By the end of his lecture I felt as confused as I had when my first girl-friend told me she loved me but wanted to break up with me. It was without a doubt one of the most boring talks of my life.

I was especially annoyed with the Digg website. Marvin's instructions on using it made me feel sick.

"You have to be careful with Digg. Remember, the top 'Diggers' are very respected because they trawl thousands of sites for the very best articles and keep their eyes open for the breaking news. You can't just join the website and throw your weight around, you have to earn trust."

So in theory, Marvin was telling me that after my career of wasting people for money, I now had to bend over, put my hands on the desk and let a team of internet freaks shaft me as hard as possible just because I wanted to spend some time outdoors and away from a computer.

"These guys don't leave their houses but they have more respect and following than an actual person who lives a real life?"

"That's correct. It's the Digg way."

"Well no offence Marvin, but I don't like the Digg way. Come on Alan, we're going."

Alan jumped up and brushed the biscuit crumbs off his jumper. We'd been there such a long time Marvin had offered a delightful selection of sugary treats.

"Marvin. Thanks for the advice but if you ever tell anyone about this I will beat the crap out of you."

I slammed the door shut. It had been a tiring and unproductive morning.

An Afternoon With Amber

I dropped Alan off and sped towards Amber's place. It was strange that I would see her merely minutes after threatening her work mate with a gun. She prepared some food for me.

"Here you are. I used the pesto sauce you like."

I ate my spaghetti and relished the peace and quiet of Amber's minimal but eloquent apartment. Recently, my head had been filled with nothing but digital marketing and for the first time in what seemed like forever I was beginning to feel like a real human person once more.

"I'll make the tea and you prepare the DVD."

It was beautiful. No talk of 'niche markets' or 'bandwidth.' All I had to do was put Arrested Development in the machine then sit back and wait for the hilarity. We watched two episodes that were both equally funny and proceeded to proceed to the nearest bar for a few drinks.

"I understand the internet, but it's not really a replacement for real life."

She spoke the truth. The internet was most definitely cool, but my recent detachment from reality was alarming. I'd even forgotten to write a postcard to my Mother. I had to see just how normal Amber was.

"Say, what are your plans for tomorrow morning? Do you have a Sunday routine?"

"Well, I enjoy a coffee and the newspapers but aside from that it's just general stuff around the house, maybe some ironing or if the weather's nice I can take a walk on the beach."

She was perfect.

I thought about all the blogs I'd been reading concerning the new wave of Sunday morning 'blogathons' where marketing experts scrapped it out online to uncover the top ten most controversial news stories and present them in a user friendly web page with media rich applications to help enhance the viewing.

 The competitor with the most votes and comments combined won a free subscription to 'Web Ethics' magazine which was a highly regarded source of information according to Jim Evans-Buckle, the CEO of 'Click and Save', a profitable affiliate marketing company that had recently merged with 'Youth Energy,' an online e-zine that used social networking to report on the latest online trends for consumers under eighteen years old.

And all Amber did on a Sunday was drink coffee and do ironing. There was only one more thing I needed to know.

"Do you listen to the radio whilst you iron?"

"Well yes, but it's just a bit of background noise."

Lock and load. I popped the question.

"Amber. Will you be my official girlfriend?"

"Oh Michael!"

She seemed happy. I held up a hand so I could continue.

"And when we're together can we do really normal things like surfing or maybe going to the shops to buy ice cream?"

"Isn't that all a bit boring for a mover and shaker like yourself?"

Amber laughed at her joke. I gave her a gentle smile.

"Maybe."

There was no maybe about it. I would get my share of normality if it was the last thing I did.

Even if I had to kill every single member of Digg.com.

Dealing With Those Freaks From Digg.com

Adam Hazard looked well. He wore a fine Armani suit and his blue eyes were kept well hidden behind a pair of sunglasses that probably cost more than the very best Dream Awake package.

"I'm not sure I understood you Michael. Just so we can be clear, please repeat what you said ten seconds ago."

Adam Hazard was naturally cocky, it was his style. Right now, I didn't have time for it.

"Come on Adam, just help me out."

"Help you out? You want me to blow up the Digg.com headquarters?"

He was right. It sounded ridiculous. Furthermore I wasn't killing anybody anymore. In fact, I hadn't killed anyone in months, except for Penelope, and that was different.

My new found morals had made me feel like a better person. Since I'd stopped killing people I'd started a business and formed a surprisingly good relationship with a nicely scented librarian who was helping me to be normal. I'd also won new friends in Josh and Cherry.

"I'm sorry Adam, I'm just fried. Running my business and trying to get my head round all this online marketing. It's a nightmare to be honest with you."

"Online marketing?"

Adam laughed and sunk the remainder of his beer. He let out a sigh and took off his shades.

"Okay Michael. This Digg.com business. You say that you can't compete with these so called 'diggers' who find all the best online information?"

"That's right. I don't know how they do it or how they have the time to do it. I get bored after ten minutes online, my eyes start to hurt."

"Well I've got a better idea and nobody has to get killed."

"Go on."

And he did. In fact, Adam came up with one of the best plans I'd ever heard.

We returned to my mansion and gave Cherry, Josh and Alan enough money for the movies. I didn't have time to babysit. Adam and I had work to do.

The aim of the plan was to locate the most respected 'digger' in the world. The rest was simple. Online humiliation.

Come Out, Come Out, Wherever You Are

His or her username was *berry_boost476*. All we discovered was that he or she was using a computer from somewhere in New York. I'd been thinking about a quick trip to the Big Apple for some new trainers so I was pleased to kill two birds with one stone.

Adam and I walked from baggage claim and hailed a cab. The streets were cold and threatening. New York was a far cry from the gentle Florida. There were no dolphins juggling beach balls out here, just fast walking, irritable civilians who had somewhere more important to be.

"Are you ready?"

Adam may have been a joker at heart, but when it came down to it, the guy was all about the job. He was focused and obviously worried my mind wasn't on the task at hand.

"Let's do this."

We threw some money at our miserable driver and marched straight towards the building we believed *berry_boost476* was holed up in.

"I'm getting a signal. He's digging right now. Follow me."

Adam was good. Intense. I followed him up the corridor. We approached the end and he signalled to the door on the right hand side, 506 A. I only hoped whoever lived in B had gone out for the day. Adam kicked the door in.

"Go, go, go!"

We moved quickly through the hall, the kitchen, and the living room until we found a single white door with blue light escaping from underneath it.

This time I was the one who went charging in, using my shoulder to splinter the door open as if it were a wet paper bag.

"Freeze you fucking nerd."

berry_boost476 was a man with curly black hair. His features were best described as mildly podgy, with a soft looking stomach gently probing against a Ramones t-shirt. He didn't have a chance to say anything as Adam leapt across the room, aiming a kick straight towards his doughy face.

berry_boost476 tipped backwards in his chair, crashing to the floor with an almighty thud. Adam grabbed him by the hair and yanked him up to his feet.

"Are you *berry_boost476?*"

"What?"

Adam slapped him round the face, causing his cheek to wobble and go a deeper shade of red.

"I asked you a simple question. Are you *berry_boost476?*"

The man gained control over his breathing.

"Yes. I'm *berry_boost476*. Please, what do you want? I haven't done anything wrong."

I stepped forward sensing my time had come.

"That's not entirely true now is it?"

I motioned for Adam to let him go.

"Now let's all sit down."

Regaining My Internet Presence

As Adam made us all coffee, I relayed my argument to Doug. This was his name. Behind the safety of *berry_boost476* lay Douglas Carmichael, a thirty-seven year old programmer who specialised in building micro sites for some established corporate clients.

"I don't have time to sit around on Digg.com all day, 'digging' or whatever the hell it is you do."

Douglas didn't flinch. He was playing hardball.

"Look Douglas. I know you're the worlds' number one 'digger.' I know that much. And that's why we're here today."

Douglas looked proud at the acknowledgement. He was a fool, but I had to give it to him, he was composed now, aware that I was leading into an argument I couldn't really understand. Douglas made his move.

"Mr. West, you can't just sign up for Digg and not contribute. Some people, such as myself, take it very seriously. You haven't even told me what your specific problem is with Digg?"

"I want the respect of the entire internet and I want everyone to come and look at my business online."

"And you thought you could just sign up for Digg and post a few links to your website, is that right?"

I couldn't see the problem with this approach. That was exactly how I'd played my cards and yet there were no more visitors to the Dream Awake site than any other day. Either way I'd had about enough of this conversation.

"Adam, set up the web cam."

Adam had been sitting observantly in the corner, ready to pounce on my instructions. This time, I wouldn't need his exceptional speed and element of surprise. I knew Douglas wasn't going anywhere.

I stood up and landed an excellent kick to his face, sending him tumbling backwards once again.

"Stop kicking me!"

"Get yourself up Doug. We've got work to do."

The first stage was the letter of resignation from Digg. Adam and I knew that coming from the worlds' number one 'digger' it would have a real impact. Of course, we wrote it, but Doug was going to sign off and post it on his very own Digg account. It was dynamite.

This is berry_boost476, you're hero. As you know, I've been digging for years and I thank you all for your support. I have however, just realised that Digg is for losers and I feel as though I've definitely wasted my time on this website, hence my decision to make this my last Digg post. As of right now I will be retiring and returning to the real world where I will be forced to interact with people on a normal and level playing field. You are all losers, and I am too.

p.s. I did find a really good site, dreamawake.com. It's a wonderful business, and I'm signing up with them.

With that out of the way we moved on to the powerful medium of online video. Whilst I had been talking to Douglas, Adam had accessed the *berry_boost476* youtube account.

Ten minutes later we had posted a video of Doug signing the Batman theme with his pants down. That alone would decrease the number of his followers significantly.

As Adam and I went through the airport en route back home, I knew I'd put an end to my online worries once and for all.

Twenty four hours later I woke up surrounded by beer bottles and an uncomfortable looking Adam Hazard who was mumbling into the phone.

"Hmmm....okay, okay, right. How bad? Okay."

I sat up and watched Adam slowly hang up.

"What's the problem?"

"You know the youtube video we made of Doug singing the Batman theme?"

It had only been a day ago, of course I remembered. I could tell this wasn't going to be good.

"What's the problem Adam?"

"The problem is that the video received over seven million views in its first hour. Youtube crashed as a result. Doug's going to be a star Michael, Larry King's already lining him up for an exclusive."

Jesus. Larry King. Doug was going to be huge. The question was whether he would let us fry or keep our involvement a secret. If I was exposed as some kind of bullying monster then it would surely be the end of Dream Awake and I'd be left with nothing but a brothel that made me millions of dollars. My dream of becoming a respected entrepreneur was on the line.

"I think this is as far as I can go Michael. You're going to have to lay low. The power of the internet will destroy you quicker than something that destroys things quickly."

I didn't stop Adam leaving. He'd been dragged around enough. It was time to face the music on my own. Ten minutes later I stood in front of Cherry, Josh and Alan.

"Okay guys, good hustle, thanks for coming."

"What's wrong Michael?"

"Shut up for a second Alan. I just need to let you all know that there may be some negative exposure about Dream Awake due to me humiliating a complete stranger who's just become really famous."

Suffering the Consequences

"Josh, Monica Stewart from the New York Times is on the phone, she wants to know if there's any truth to the allegations made on Larry King last night."

Just as I'd expected Doug had gone on air and told the entire story of his abduction at the hands of Adam and I. He'd left no detail out and somehow he'd managed to sign a two year deal with HBO for his own comedy show themed around the batman segment of his youtube video.

"Michael?"

Cherry looked irritated. Poor thing, dragged off the streets, given a great business, only to have it all taken away as a result of my hidden urge to bully someone fat.

"I'm coming, I'm coming."

I shuffled apologetically past Cherry and made my way to the study where the phone lay there like a landmine.

"This is Michael West."

"Michael. Monica Stewart, New York Times."

"Hi there Monica, how are you?"

"Is there any truth to the fat guys' story?"

I thought about it long and hard. A lot could change depending on the answer I gave her. The truth? Or the lie?

"None whatsoever Monica, it is an outrageous accusation and I fully intend to fight this all the way."

Not Suffering the Consequences

I sat nervously in my aisle seat. Like Josh, flying had never been a big thing for me and now I was on my way to New York. Again.

Cherry, Alan and Josh had agreed to put things on hold during the publicity and I paid them back by giving them free reign of my house, parties included in the deal. It was the least I could do to the people who were now like family to me, and I tried not to think about what would happen if I lost everything we'd worked so hard for.

Alan would no doubt return to his office and be an accountant, but I'd completely interrupted the lives of Josh and Cherry. Technically I'd saved their lives but in some ways dying might have been less hassle for them.

Monica's office was just like I'd imagined, spacious, luxurious and with a cookie like aroma that was no doubt intended to make her visitors let their guard down. An intern breezed in with a pot of coffee and a stack of papers.

"Thank you Rachel," quipped Monica without taking her gaze off me.

I would have to be careful, you didn't get this far in New York without having a nasty bite. After what seemed like an eternity, Monica looked away and assembled some recording equipment before pouring us both a coffee.

"Michael, if you work with me, we're going to have your name cleared in no time at all. I want to set up an exclusive ready for publication by next weekend."

"That's in two days Monica," I said, not quite sure of whether such a feat was possible.

"Precisely. Not only will your enemies be caught by surprise, but we will paint such a good picture of you it will be a traditional double punch."

She was good. She was very good.

"Then let's get to work."

I wasn't naïve. I knew that this valiant piece of journalism was going to cost me, and I was ready. In my spare hour off the plane I'd checked into the hotel, showered and even got a hair-cut for $100.

This woman was going to have the night of passion she so sorely craved, and I was going to be a big shot businessman once again.

Three hours later and we were sipping champagne on my balcony. I ran a hand through Monica's hair which was so blonde it almost lit up the busy Manhattan streets below.

"I've had a great time with you Monica. I wish it didn't have to end."

"It doesn't Michael."

And that was when Amber, my brilliantly normal girlfriend, popped into my head. My previously awesome situation had become decidedly un-cool, and I tried to weigh up the options.

1. Stay in New York with the Queen of the press who was also devastatingly hot in a powerful kind of way.

2. Return to Florida to the pleasant and safe Amber

and the three very different people knocking about
in my mansion.

I realised how nervous I felt imagining my high profile life in New York
with Monica. It would be an endless stream of wine bars and sophisticated friends called Charles or Charlotte. At least with Amber I'd be
able to watch television on a Friday night.

It had to be Amber.

"I'm sure we'll be able to see more of each other Monica, but I have a
life in Florida that I can't just run away from."

She leaned forward and kissed me, slipping out of her silk robe.

"You take all the time you want Michael. I'm not going anywhere."

And so I performed as expected for the flattering article soon to be hitting the news. I had to admit, I'd landed on my feet on this occasion.

*Innocent and Scared- how Michael West is dealing with becoming the
worlds latest figure of hate.*

Story by Monica Stewart.

*"All my life I've just wanted to fit in but there's a part of me that just doesn't
feel accepted."*

*Michael West is no ordinary businessman. Growing up with little money,
he's been gifted with a strong work ethic from his mother, Betty West.*

*"She always told me that for every problem I had, there were thousands of
people who had it worse and needed help."*

*Perhaps this is the inspiration behind Michael's business 'Dream Awake', a
controversial real life fantasy world which allows anyone to live their dream*

for a price. There are no limits, as sixteen year old Tommy Bass discovered when he was called up for the Boston Red Sox last month.

"Yeah I remember Tommy. He nearly died in a freak boating accident and his father wanted to give him a really special day. $700,000 later and little Tommy's putting on the batting helmet in front of thousands of screaming fans. It was really something."

But despite making Tommy's dreams and many others come true, it seems Michael can't shake off his doubters. There have been accusations of brothels, drug abuse and even murder. More recently, we've had to sit back and watch the over played youtube clip of the now famous berry_boost476, who sang the batman theme with his pants down.

Earlier this month, Michael was accused of breaking into Douglas Carmichael's home and subjecting him to verbal and physical abuse in an apparent act of rage over the information sharing website Digg.com. Mr. Carmichael has even accused Michael of forcing him to write the famous Digg entry that promoted Dream Awake.

"In no way am I capable of bringing harm to another human being. I grew up with an abusive father myself, and if I could take one lesson from that experience it's that violence solves nothing."

Michael politely declined to discuss the murder trial of his father in which he was initially held as the key suspect. Rumours regarding his previous life as a contract killer have only made him more wary when it comes to trusting others.

"I think that sometimes the world is just out to get you. It doesn't make sense and it isn't fair but after a while you just have to accept the way things are. I'm more than comfortable with the way I live my life and I have a handful of wonderful friends who provide a great deal of support for me."

And is there a Mrs. West in sight?

"Ha ha. Look, it's never easy running an incredibly successful business and having a love life but that's the beauty of the world we live in today. You never know what's around the corner!"

And with that, Michael West is off to enjoy his evening. I found myself wondering if there were any other disarmingly honest and sensitive men left in the Big Apple. I know a whole host of girls who'd like to meet him.

The Return of Dream Awake

Business was booming. Monica's little piece had the phones ringing off the hook and we found ourselves swamped in work. Cherry quickly took on three new members of staff who set up shop in my garden shed which had been converted into a tidy little studio with all the mod cons.

Doug Carmichael's career was stalling. His show had been cancelled after just one season, and I had no doubt that Monica's work was the direct result of it. Larry King had lost a million viewers overnight simply by having Doug in for an interview.

Adam Hazard found it incredibly amusing, but he wasn't tempted to return to Florida, I think those few weeks had felt like a few years for him and he took his down time very seriously.

"Michael can I have a word please?"

It was Alan. I wasn't too happy about the interruption as day dreaming had always been a thing for me but I knew that as my employee I needed to treat his problems even more seriously than mine.

"Alan, you look great today. Come in and have a seat. How's your wife?"

"I'm erm, I'm still divorced Micahel."

Knickers. I never seemed to learn.

"Well let's not worry about that Alan, what's new?"

"Well, I feel a little odd saying this Michael, but it's Josh."

"What about him?"

I'd always though Josh and Alan got on well with each together. This gave me a bad feeling. Alan rarely said anything, but when he did it was normally in the form of a problem he had.

"Well, you see…I'd been hoping to…er……hoping to ask Cherry if maybe she would like a drink with me one night."

"Wow, really? That's great Alan."

This was not great at all. First off Alan stood no chance with Cherry and secondly, his broken heart was going to cost me an accountant.

"Well, I can't act on my feelings Michael because I think that Josh is trying to…."

"You think Josh is interested in Cherry? That's ridiculous! Excuse me one sec Alan."

I rushed out of the office pretending to take an important call on my cell phone. Two minutes later I found Josh rummaging through the freezer.

"Michael, we're out of ice-cream."

"Josh, forget that, you need to do me a favour, I haven't got much time."

"Whatever you need Michael. What's the problem?"

"Don't ask me why, just stop hitting on Cherry or dating her if that's what your doing."

Josh had a knowing look on his face.

"This is because of Alan isn't it? Like he has a chance! Come on Michael, that's not fair. He's got a girlfriend!"

"I know Josh, I know. I of all people understand what it's like when you've got a hot girl in your sights but please, until I think of something can you just lay off a while?"

Josh looked unconvinced.

"Josh, I'm begging you."

He dropped his shoulders and sighed.

"You got it Michael. I'll busy myself and avoid Cherry. I think she likes me though."

I laughed and clapped him on the shoulder.

"I'm sure she does kiddo, I'm sure she does."

Out of breath, I arrived back to the office where Alan was still playing with the rubix cube.

"Sorry about that champ. Important call. Now where were we? Cherry. Yes, she is one fine looking girl Alan, and I don't blame you for your concerns. I'd be super paranoid with a go get 'em guy like Josh roaming, but I really don't think you have to worry."

"Why not?"

"Josh is gay."

Alan dropped the rubix cube.

"Really?"

"Hey, if he were any gayer I'd be issuing you with a rape alarm, so I don't think you need worry about the whole Cherry situation."

"Thanks Michael, I can't tell you how relieved I am."

"No problem Alan. Run along now, I've got a mountain of paperwork."

Alan left and I typed Josh a quick e mail.

Act gay, will explain later. Thx. Michael.

My years of killing still enabled me to make snap decisions under pressure. I'd handled this one brilliantly, Josh was too out of his depth to refuse my orders and Alan was far too much of a chicken shit to actually make a move on Cherry. It was win-win.

There was a knock at the door. It was Cherry.

"Cherry, how are you?"

"Hi Michael, have you got a minute."

"I've always got a minute for you Cherry, you know that."

She strode across the room and sat down opposite me, cutting a stark contrast to the nervy accountant who had occupied the seat minutes earlier.

"How are you? I mean, after New York and everything you must be exhausted."

"Well it's been a tough few weeks for all of us Cherry, I don't think anyone is unaware of that. We pulled through though, and if anything like this happens again, we'll come out on top just like we always do."

"You didn't really break in to that guy's house and beat him up did you?"

Crap. I couldn't lose Cherry. Then again, I wondered if I'd ever had her. She was always so distant yet a brilliant business woman but I was never sure where I stood with her. Sometimes I felt the only reason Cherry carried on without complaint was out of gratitude for me saving her life.

"Cherry, I would never do that. Not to anyone."

"Okay then."

"Okay? You seem tense, let's have a drink, it's after five in the afternoon!"

Poor girl. All she needed was some reassurance every once in a while. I'd been a fool, forgetting how hard her previous life must have been, unable to trust anyone, constantly risking your life with some sex crazed freak. I reached into my fridge for a couple of light beers, feeling the warm sensation of the worlds' problems slowly evaporating into nothingness.

"Light beer for a light…"

I stopped dead in my tracks. Cherry was naked.

"Cherry….what…"

"Don't say anything Michael. I've been in love with you ever since you pointed your gun at me."

"I was going to kill you."

"But you didn't. And I don't think you ever would."

She moved closer, and I put the beers down on the desk. Any lingering thoughts of Josh and Alan vanished as she took me in her warm embrace, pushing me back on the very desk I'd purchased with the money paid to kill her.

I had to be the worlds' worst boss.

The Mind-Set of a Player

So I had three attractive women on the go and I was fairly confident all three were in love with me. All this had happened unexpectedly, just as people tell you it will. The only difference is that those people are usually talking about finding one girl and not three. As with every problem, which this situation was believe it or not, I made a list summarising my options.

Amber: Lives nearby, wonderfully normal, caring and good in bed.

Cherry: Lives in my house, pursued by other two housemates, possibly psychologically un-hinged, brilliant employee, hot.

Monica: Sophisticated, power figure of New York, sexy, saved my business.

They were all wonderful in their own way and I honestly had no desire to hurt any of them. And that was when I realised it. I'd become a complete player. All those hip hop records and television shows like Entourage were making sense to me now. I had joined the family.

To celebrate my new found status I started hitting the bars with other real life players like Sam De Brito, Neil Strauss and David De Angelo.

It was a truly great time, business by day, pleasure by night. I was even offered my own publishing contract to share some of my secrets but of course I had no interest in that game seeing as I'd decided to keep my new found status under wraps from Amber, Cherry and Monica.

I was moving on in years, and the time was coming when one of them would have to become my wife.

My weekends were divided between dinners with Monica in Manhattan, movies and take away at Amber's place and wild sex games in my own office with Cherry.

One night after a particularly heavy session, Neil Strauss brought up the subject again. At that moment in time, I was ready to agree to anything. His offer was clear enough to me.

"Write a book Michael. Write a book and tell these poor people how you became a multi-millionaire business man who spends all his non working hours having sex with beautiful women."

"I'll do it Neil. I'll do it."

I passed out in a haze of glory. The sound of the trash being collected was too far away to interrupt my glorious slumber.

The following morning I met Amber for coffee. She had been texting me a little more than usual and I felt that my lack of commitment was becoming an issue.

"I hardly see you anymore Michael."

I was right. Amber was also right. This was a tricky situation.

"Amber, you know how busy I've been. I'm really sorry that everything's come up just when we were starting to have something together."

"Well what does that mean Michael? I mean, it sounds like you're breaking up with me."

I could see the tears forming behind those beautiful eye-balls. As awesome as my life had been lately I didn't want to stop seeing her. Despite all my ambitions of sleeping with loads of women, there was a big part of me that realised I should have been doing that in my twenties and that this was not the time to throw away the best chance I'd ever have of happiness.

I decided to try and go with the best of both worlds.

"Amber, I'm going to write a book about seducing women, but it's purely a business deal. It's going to be released as part of a Dream Awake bonus package."

"Seducing women?"

I laughed out loud. A little too loud.

"I know right? It's ridiculous, but Josh tells me that's where the market is right now and its wide open for us to make a little more money. I know how you hate to hear me talk like some drab business man but this is our future we're talking about."

That did the trick. It wasn't really a trick but it was a little white lie that enabled me to keep a special lady and sleep with less special but astoundingly sexy other ladies.

"But don't you feel like you're living a lie? You're putting all this energy into something you don't believe in."

I resisted questioning Amber on how much she believed in stacking books at the library but her intelligence wasn't making my general untruths any easier.

"Come on Amber. Isn't everyone a liar in some way? Aren't we all selling ourselves each and every day? If you're going to analyse everything then of course there will be holes to find."

The next twenty minutes went a little better and we parted on good terms. I knew I had a decision to make very soon, but at that point in time I could only think about the book. I'd already decided who was going to write a review which meant another trip to New York for an evening of wine and dine.

The Offer and Confession

I'll never forget the morning of my birthday. It was the very morning I discovered just how powerful media hype can be. The phone call that I answered turned out to be the turning point of the rest of my life.

"Hi there Michael, this is Ronald Dump. You probably know who I am."

Ronald Dump was without any shadow of a doubt the most prominent businessman in America. At the age of thirteen he'd bought and sold his first stock, making a profit of three thousand dollars. It had been plain sailing ever since. He owned most of the real estate in New York, including the really big building everyone tried to buy and the wonderful apartments that over looked Central Park.

"Ronald, this comes as quite shock."

The voice on the other end of the line remained calm.

"Michael, I'm interested in making an offer on Dream Awake if you'd consider making a sale. Excuse me for being abrupt but I'm willing to go close to one hundred million dollars."

Considering I'd started the business with less than one million dollars this was quite an offer. It also gave me a nice little way out of the hole

I'd dug myself into. I'd become rich, and have all the time in the world to write my dating book. Not only that, but the others would be rich too, ready to embark on a new journey with their new lives. What a journey.

"I accept Ronald."

The voice on the other end sounded surprised.

"I..I didn't make an official offer Michael, what do you accept?"

Damn. I could have priced myself out of a lot more money.

"One hundred and twenty million dollars buys you Dream Awake."

"I'll call my lawyers Michael. I suggest you do the same. It's been a pleasure. I look forward to meeting you."

I started laughing on the phone. It was unprofessional but I couldn't help myself.

"Everything okay Michael?"

Pulling myself together I put on my best business voice.

"I'm sorry Ronald. I just saw a cat chasing a dog outside."

"I love it when that happens. Great minds think alike Michael."

"They sure do Ronald. Good to speak to you."

"Thanks Michael. Congratulations, you're life just changed."

As I hung up I took a deep breath and thought about that closing statement. I'd just cashed out my hand and walked out of the rat race. It had been a little too easy.

I assembled the team in the living room and got straight to the point.

"Okay everybody. That was Ronald Dump. He's going to pay one hundred and twenty million dollars for Dream Awake. I want to split it equally between us all."

There were gasps, open mouths and attempts to speak. Seeing as I had them on the ropes, I took my chance.

"I'm going to take my money and write a book on dating. Cherry and I have been having sex for the last four weeks. Cherry, I'm thinking about settling down with Amber. Josh and Alan, I'm sorry about going behind your backs. Alan, Josh isn't gay and you don't stand a chance with Cherry."

I exhaled and collapsed into a chair. No one had reacted.

"Come on guys, we all just made thirty million dollars. Lighten up."

And with that, the smiles started. There was a little tension in the air that was possibly due to my speech that mentioned Cherry and myself but I felt that at this stage it was time for everyone to wake up and smell the coffee.

This wasn't a playground love triangle, or whatever it is when there's four people involved. It was a story of courage, bravery and hard work that had netted us a lot of Uncle Sam.

The Party

That weekend the celebrations started. I met with Ronald Dump and his team of lawyers and the funds were transferred. We'd all worked together to ensure that the systems were installed at Dump headquarters and all business had been officially moved away from my mansion.

Josh, Cherry, Alan and I had a private dinner at the local Thai restaurant, where we spoke candidly about our plans for the future.

Saturday night was the big one. I'd organised an all out party chez moi. Harvey was there with his entourage. Sam De Brito, Neil Strauss and David De Angelo all turned up but I had given them strict instructions about running game on my female guests. I wanted to have a civilised few hours before the naughty stuff began.

Overall there were around one hundred guests, and I was having a nightmare keeping the bathrooms in order. My hired help seemed to be spending most of their time eating and drinking with the crowd but what did I care? Thirty million tends to eliminate a lot of concerns.

"Hey you."

I turned round in shock. How long had I been looking at myself in the mirror? Why hadn't I locked the bathroom door?

"I've been looking for you."

It was Cherry. She didn't forget to lock the door, moving towards me as she slid out of her silk gown.

"You know Michael, there are many things that turn a woman on but nothing comes close to brutal honesty."

She grabbed hold of me and planted one of her world famous kisses on my lips.

"I think it's cute that you've made a little plan with Amber, but we all know it's just a phase."

"Cherry. I don't know what to say."

"So don't Michael. You know we're meant to be together, we built this business and made it what it is."

She tried to kiss me again. I gently pulled back.

"Cherry, you know how much I value you. But I'm serious about Amber. I really think I might have something with her."

I desperately wanted to sleep with Cherry, but something in my head kept telling me to do the right thing.

"We've been fucking for a month Michael. Just what is it you have with Amber that's so special?"

Our conversation was interrupted by screaming from downstairs. We both ran downstairs to see what the commotion was about. A very drunk and handsome man grabbed hold of me.

"He just went crazy, it all started as a joke. Then they were swinging at each other!"

I scanned the room until I saw what I least expected to see. Josh was impaled by a fire poker. He was very much dead. People were screaming. There was a little blood escaping across the floor. The closest man to Josh with the guiltiest face was Alan.

"Jesus Christ Alan, what did you do?"

"It was an accident!"

Alan started to cry. I started to think. Most of my guests started to leave.

"Alan, take his body and drag it out to the garden. You need to bury him right now."

"What about…what….the police…Michael. The police."

"You want to give them a call Alan?"

The house had emptied. I had no idea if anyone had called the police. That was when I thought of who I needed to call. There was no need.

"It seems like you could use my help Michael. I always knew you'd kill him eventually."

"Not funny Harvey. He was a good boy."

"A good boy who enjoyed playing with fire. How ironic that his death is the result of a fire poker."

I was not amused. Harvey continued regardless.

"Michael, get in the car and drive as far away as possible. Take your team with you."

"What are you going to do?"

"You don't need to know just now. Right now you've got no other choice."

I knew he was right. We all had our money, and this ridiculous death stunt by Josh wasn't going to change anything. Except maybe the rest of Alan's life but that was his problem.

"Alan, Cherry. Get in the car. We're leaving."

The car journey was awkward to say the least. Alan was crying about both killing Josh and losing any chance he had with Cherry. Cherry was deathly silent next to me in the front seat which I knew was a bad sign, and I wasn't able to get hold of Harvey to find out what was happening back at the mansion.

Two hours later and we had arrived at the anonymous looking motel I had in mind.

"We've all had a long night and nothing we say right now is going to change anything. Let's get ourselves together, check in and have a stiff drink or whatever it takes to help us relax a little."

Alan was still sobbing.

"Alan, you have got to get it together."

Cherry still hadn't flinched. I decided better than to ask her how she was. Our bathroom conversation was just heating up when the whole Josh being dead incident occurred.

"Right, here's some money you two, head inside and clean up. I'm going to sort out the car."

At that point Cherry broke her silence.

"I think my coats in the back Michael. Can you get it for me? I'm going to have a cigarette."

"Fine. Alan, head inside. It's freezing out here, we'll meet you there."

Alan slumped out of the car and towards the motel. I ambled to the trunk and opened it up to find Cherry's mink coat and Amber's dead body. I practically lost my footing and stumbled back in disbelief.

"You didn't really think it was just going to end that easily did you Michael?"

Cherry was out of the car now, calmly smoking her cigarette.

"Cherry..what have you done?"

"My entire life has been spent performing one degrading act after another for child like men to get their rocks off. Then one day, someone like you comes along and makes me realise there are still real men out there. I'm not letting go of you Michael. Take care of me and I'll take care of you."

If only she knew the half of it. Now I had the tough call to make. Was it going to be necessary to take Cherry out? Was she a threat? Should I reward her obvious dedication to me by making her my wife? I couldn't really call her a monster for killing Amber. It would be hypocritical to say the least.

"Let's get rid of the body."

It had been a traumatic two hours but we eventually put Amber six feet under in the nearby forest area. I was exhausted from all the digging and had been surprised at Cherry's stamina. She was a real trooper alright. I doubted if Amber would have managed ten minutes if the roles were reversed.

"We'd better go and check on Alan."

We headed back to the motel and knocked on the door of Alan's room. With no answer, I entered at my own accord and found Alan huddled up in bed watching cartoons.

"Slide up big guy, we're here for you."

Cherry nudged me in the back. I turned abruptly and whispered angrily in her ear.

"Just climb in the bed and snuggle up, we can't have any more freak-outs tonight."

And so the three of us lay together in the master bed with the gentle hum of the television in the background. Alan remained in the foetal position sucking his thumb as Cherry spooned him, and I spooned Cherry from the other side. As weird as it was it turned out to be a wonderfully therapeutic night.

The next morning I checked in with Harvey who had taken care of everything in its entirety.

There would be no witnesses, no body and officially no such party took place at my mansion. It had been cleaned and looked good as new. In return he wanted six months free services from both Dream Awake and the brothel which I duly agreed to without hesitation, pending a long call to Ronald Dump.

There was a message from Monica informing me that there may be some reports of her being seen on a date with a well known sports star. On any other day it might have bothered me but I'd already lost a friend and the woman I believed I was going to settle down with. I wanted things back to normal, the nine to five working days.

One Week Later

Back at the mansion I'd already put things back on track.

I arranged a fantastic team of counsellors for Alan and set him up with a busy timetable of exercise, excursions and free use of the brothel. Although I worried about him never fully recovering from being a killer, I at least hoped to make his life easier nonetheless.

Harvey hadn't been lying, the mansion was spotless and all signs of that tragic night were long gone. Cherry and I held a memorial service for Josh in the garden which was very emotional. He had been such a brilliant employee and despite escaping the murderous clutches of Harvey all those months ago had finally met his fate because of a different girl.

It was almost as if women had been put on the earth to keep brilliant men like Josh from living a full and productive life.

And so it was just Cherry and I. How did I feel about it? I couldn't tell you. I sure missed Amber, but I'd become a great believer in fate and making things even brighter was the fact that Cherry was in full support of my plans to write my book containing the ultimate pick up secrets for men.

She'd actually become quite close to my three buddies Sam De Brito, Neil Strauss and David De Angelo.

The best thing about it was that all three of them persistently tried to sleep with her, but I was the one she came home to every night. When we had sex Cherry would constantly tell me about them hitting on her which I found to be a real turn on. Yes indeed, my life could have been a lot worse.

Ronald Dump had phoned me once every week just to let me know how everything was going with Dream Awake. I found that to be a really professional touch. Cherry was also thinking about selling up the House of Discretion, our fantastic brothel that was still running since the sale of Dream Awake.

"If we give up the House of Discretion what are you going to do?"

I wanted to be sure Cherry had some direction in her life.

"Michael, I've told you already. You write your book and I'll sell it. I learned so much from Josh and this arrangement gives us the chance to spend time together. Unless that's not what you want?"

Yes Cherry still had it. I felt an overwhelming attraction to this woman who every man wanted yet had no idea how desperately she wanted to be wanted. It was perfect.

Amber's demise was saddening to the core, but I'd always been a believer in the theory that we had not one soul mate but a potential ten thousand, scattered across the globe. Those who thought otherwise were simply lonely people, setting themselves up for heartbreak again and again.

So what did I learn by not killing people? (except for Madam Penelope)

I learnt that each and every one of us has a way in which to contribute to the greater cause. Whether it's basic numeracy, sales or people skills you'd be surprised at what someone can do if you just trust them enough to do it.
Years of killing and rudeness have created what I like to call the 'Shit effect' which is how I'd some up many places in the world, especially England. The 'Shit effect' represents everything from rude receptionists, to drunk twats who have nothing better to do that start trouble.

So the next time you meet someone, don't think about killing them. Ask questions, be interested and find out who that special person is just waiting to burst out.

Epilogue

Michael West continues life as a successful entrepreneur. He currently resides in Los Angeles with his wife Katie 'Cherry' Deline and their dog Heidi.

The infamous House of Discretion was snapped up by Ronald Dump, now a close friend of both Michael and Katie.

Michael and Katie are now heavily involved in the production of Michael's up coming book, "Why I pick up great chicks and you don't."